Daniel Lee
FINDING DAD

illustrated by Korky Paul

For Paula, Ben and Rebecca.
Without them, there would be no book.
D.L.

For all prisoners' families
K.P.

DANIEL LEE (b1962), started out writing lyrics and music for various bands. His Mum liked his writing, so he studied journalism, wrote for magazines and newspapers and, in the mid 1990s, he worked at *The Guardian* in London.

Since then, Daniel has penned books for Channel 4 on an array of subjects, from inventions to run-away children, and he has written various works of fiction. He has continued writing for *The Guardian*, as well as *The Times* and the *Evening Standard*. His Mum still thinks he can write.

KORKY PAUL (b1951) grew up scribbling in Zimbabwe and studied Fine Art and Film Animation. He started work in advertising.

He has illustrated the "Winnie The Witch" books by Valerie Thomas, winner of the Children's Book Award. Korky has illustrated several other books for Oxford, Penguin, and Random House including anthologies of poems edited by John Foster and Michael Rosen.

He is known (only to himself) as the world's greatest dinosaur portrait artist.

Foreword

In 2004, more than 175,000 people were sent to prison in England & Wales, leaving behind them children, partners and parents to cope with the aftermath of their imprisonment. This meant that 150,000 children lost a mum or dad, in circumstances that they had no control over and many may not have been told the truth about where their parent had gone.

In total, an estimated 7% of the school population in England & Wales (approximately 600,000 children) will experience the imprisonment of their parent during their time in school. For some of these children, having a prisoner in the family may almost be considered 'normal' within the community. For others, it will be a traumatic experience, well outside the norm. Yet all of them, along with their families, face issues of trust, stigma and possible isolation. The impact of imprisonment on children can be extremely damaging and many experience some of the following changes: Becoming withdrawn or secretive; displaying anger or defiance (especially against authority figures such as teachers); attention-seeking or self-destructive behaviour, poor educational performance; and significant mental health problems.

We also know that many children do not want to tell their friends or teachers what has happened in case they are treated differently, bullied or teased. Some parents decide to 'protect' their children from the truth and make up stories about where their dad, or mum, has gone. In general though, children want to be told the truth - only then can they understand what has happened.

Action for Prisoners' Families commissioned *Finding Dad* to raise awareness of these issues and to help children of prisoners to know that they are not alone; that their situation can and does happen to many other children; and that they can still care about their parent in prison and keep in contact with them. I hope you will enjoy the story and take a moment to think about those children with a mum or dad in prison.

Lucy Gampell
Director, Action for Prisoners' Families

Acknowledgements

Action for Prisoners' Families would like to thank all those who inspired and encouraged us to produce this book. Particular thanks go to the following children and young people who reviewed the first draft of the book – Abigail, Archie, Ben, Rebecca, Edward, Gideon, Megan & Oliver. We are especially grateful to the Ormiston Children & Families Trust and to Miss Katherine Cowpe and the children in Year 3C at Barnes Primary School for market-testing the book and giving us such useful feedback, without all their enthusiasm and positive comments, dad may have been lost forever!

Our special thanks go to Korky Paul, who so generously donated his time to illustrate *Finding Dad* and to Daniel Lee for all his work in bringing the ideas to life.

Finally Action for Prisoners' Families would like to thank Emily Guille-Marratt for editing the book and Bird & Bird for donating their professional advice.

Action for Prisoners' Families Published by Action for Prisoners' Families

With thanks to the Nationwide Foundation for funding this publication

First published in Great Britain in 2005
Designed by Nicola Kenwood @ Hakoona Matata Designs

Text © Daniel Lee 2005
Illustrations © Korky Paul 2005
The moral right of the author has been asserted

Charity Registration Number: 267879

Printed in the United Kingdom by Masterprint

Contents

CHAPTER 1
Dad disappears..11

CHAPTER 2
Teacher's pet...22

CHAPTER 3
Secrets..33

CHAPTER 4
A mystery trip...50

CHAPTER 5
From Brazil to Burpy Brad............................68

CHAPTER 6
The truth...92

CHAPTER 7
A run for my life..111

CHAPTER 1
Dad disappears

Dad is very brave, Mum is always telling me. I have never been sure what she meant, but that's about to change. Everything is about to change. The baby blackbirds chirping in a nest in the holly bush outside my bedroom window woke me up and now I can't sleep. They look like monster aliens or skinny frozen-chicken legs. I tried to feed them bits of bread once, but Dad told me I might frighten them.

I'd like to watch the chicks all day and I'm thinking of ways to stay off school. Shall I pretend to be ill? Shall I have a tummy ache? No. The last time I did that Mum took me to the doctor and I had to take some horrible, yellowy-green medicine. It was like a magic potion. Just thinking about its bitter taste makes me roll myself tighter and tighter into the safety of my warm, space-rocket duvet. Maybe I should have a headache instead.

Before I can do anything about my plans for a day at home, there's a loud knock at the front door. All the chicks go quiet and I hear Mum and Dad rushing around in their bedroom and then Mum runs downstairs.

"Good morning," a bossy-sounding man's voice says, as the front door squeaks open. "Are you

Rachel McDonald?" the man asks.

"Yes," Mum replies, but as she is about to say something else the man carries on talking.

"Is David Orchard home?"

Why is this man asking for Dad so early in the morning? Before Mum can tell him anything, I hear Dad go to the door. "Yes," Dad says. Then the voices go quieter. I keep listening to the noise of people talking, but I can't understand what they are saying. Their voices sound like listening to next door's telly through the wall. Now they are all shouting and I am getting annoyed because I still can't understand what they are saying.

When Mum and Dad are having what they call their "private chats" they don't like me going down, so I stay in my bed. I listen to these strange voices for what seems like

ages and I can't stop myself creeping to the top of the stairs to try and see what is happening. My little sister Jody is already there. She looks at me and whispers, "What's going on?"

"I don't know," I snap back. When I answer, all the adults downstairs stop talking. "Are the children up?" Mum asks, angrily. Jody and I quickly and quietly duck out of sight.

"No, it's all still dark up there," Dad says and they carry on talking.

Phew! That was close. It's like one of the secret agent games I used to play with Dad, but now it seems to be for real.

There must be ten policemen and women squashed into our little house. Something big must be happening. They are looking around at everything, poking their noses round doors and watching Dad really carefully. One of them, a tall, fat man wearing a squashed hat, seems to be stuck in the front door. He does most of the talking.

After a while of listening at the top of the stairs, I begin to make out a few more words. The police keep calling Dad "sir". Mum must have told them how important and brave he is. She's always telling me. Then the policeman with the squashed hat starts talking about a "big operation". With all the noise and other people talking it is difficult to be certain, but I think he says, "this is one of our biggest operations and you would be well-advised to help us, sir".

I can just see a policewoman with her arm round Mum. Mum seems to be upset and crying, but she must know the policewoman really well because they are having a really big hug. She seems to give her a bit of a squeeze as Dad walks out of the front door. One of the policemen helps Dad into a police car. All the police get back in their cars and speed off so fast that their wheels skid and start to smoke. It's like watching a TV car chase and all our neighbours stare out of their windows. I can tell they think Dad is ace. I feel really proud of him. He must be off to do something very important.

Now I know why Dad has been in a mood for the past few weeks. He must have been busy thinking about helping the police with their big operation. When he's busy he often stops listening to me and if I keep trying to talk to him he gets angry. When he is in one of his really horrible moods, I hide in my bedroom and imagine I am somewhere else until he goes out. One of my favourite places to imagine myself, is on a ship sailing to Africa on a sunny sea. But I don't think Dad is always horrible. He isn't. He bought me football pyjamas the other day. He can be a laugh.

Last week, Dad took Jody and me fishing on the river. We pretended we were on a desert-island adventure and we had to get all our own food. "Watch out for the people in the woods," he warned. "They'll creep out, capture you and force you to eat ant-heads with squashed worms." We all kept checking anything that came from the woods. When we heard twigs breaking, we all ran and hid. Then a man walked out with his dog and he looked at us as if we were mad.

We were there for hours and we

didn't catch any fish.

"Better get back to the castle," Dad said. Even though our house is really small he still calls it our castle. He always says, "Don't forget to pull up the draw bridge," when we get in and close the front door. On the way home after our trip to the river we bought two fish from the supermarket so Mum would think we caught them.

"Well done," she said. "You must have spent ages getting these fish so clean!"

As Mum took the fish off the table, Dad turned to me and Jody and whispered, "I think we tricked her."

Another time, at my eighth birthday party, not long ago, my Dad made all my friends laugh when he pretended to be an astronaut. It was in the Easter holidays. He walked very slowly across the kitchen, pretending he was floating in space and I was the scientist in charge of the base station on Earth.

"Calling J," he said, holding his hand over his mouth and acting as if he had a radio. He's always calling me J. My real name is James Orchard, but most people call me Jimmy. "J, are you there?" he said. I did feel a bit silly, but I enjoyed it. It was fun. Even Jody laughed. At her last birthday party when she was six he pretended to be a ballet dancer and that was even sillier.

You see, we do have a good time together, but now he's off on a job and Mum is upset we won't be having any fun until he gets back. After Dad speeds off in the police car, Mum disappears into the bathroom for a long time. She often does that when she's upset.

"What's going on?" Jody asks me again.

"I don't know, but I do know we have to find Dad," I reply.

I want to have a good time with him again, for him to give me one of his bear hugs and tell me a joke. But first I have to find him and the more I think about where he might be, the more I feel lost.

CHAPTER 2

Teacher's pet

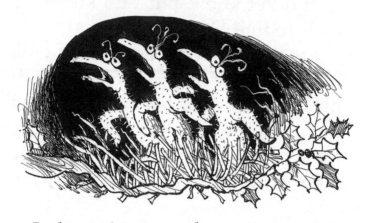

Jody and I sit on the stairs outside the bathroom for ages trying to think of a way to find Dad. When Mum finally comes out of the bathroom she doesn't seem any better. She is still upset and starts to order us around like we are in the army. "Jody. Jimmy. Down for breakfast. Now. We're late for school."

We both rush down to the kitchen. "Where's Dad gone?" Jody asks.

"It's a secret," Mum snaps back.

"If you tell us, we won't tell anyone," I say.

"He's on a secret mission helping the government. Leave it at that, Jimmy," Mum says.

We all sit and eat breakfast quietly, except Mum's not really eating. She is just fiddling with her food, staring at the table and pushing her toast from one side of the plate to the other. What's wrong with her? No one speaks. All I can hear is the disgusting sound of Jody and me chewing our food. We sound like two camels eating cake. Yuk.

Jody and I are still munching on our cereal when Mum rushes us out of the house for school. I hate being rushed out of the house in the morning. When we get to school, the teachers all keep asking us if we are alright. "If you want a chat any time, please come and see me," Mr

Stunkin says. He's normally really horrible and short-tempered. "You're a dreamer, James," he's usually shouting at me. "You prefer to live in your head rather than in the real world," he's always saying. But not now. Now he's being all nice. Well, I'd rather spend my day in my head than in a classroom with him.

If I was going to talk with someone, it wouldn't be Mr Stunkin. Everyone calls him Mr Stinkin behind his back because his breath smells. Then Miss Tadey also asks if I want to talk. People think her voice sounds like a steam engine and her eyes stick out like a toad's, so you can guess what they call her. Anyway, whatever they say, I like her. She's my teacher and she's always nice to me. But that doesn't mean I want to tell her anything. If I start talking with her too much people will think I'm teacher's pet. Why would I ever want to talk with a teacher, even if they haven't got smelly breath or they don't look like a friendly toad?

The morning goes so slowly it feels more like a whole week. At lunch break I tell Ahmed how annoyed I'm getting that everyone keeps making such a fuss. He's in my class and we always play together. Sometimes we sneak toys into school so we can play with them in the playground. He only listens for a few seconds before telling me about some new toys he got for his birthday. "They're really good," he says, "just like the warriors out of *Lord of the Rings*."

"Great," I reply, trying to pretend I'm interested. Usually I would want him to tell me more, but today nothing seems very interesting. All I can think about is Dad's secret mission. I bet he's having a fantastic adventure somewhere helping the government. And I'm stuck here at school. It's not fair. Luckily Jack, from year three, plays one of his legendary jokes on the head teacher, Mrs Grampy (who everyone calls Grumpy), or the day would seem even longer. Jack's always playing jokes. He always gets into trouble, but it doesn't seem to make any difference.

Today Jack sets a trap in the corridor for Grumpy. He attaches a piece of string to a fire hose so that when she steps on it, the hose squirts her. Grumpy is soaked and so are some other teachers. "Jack Drake," Grumpy screams. "You're in big trouble, now." She always blames him, because he is almost always to blame. Jack's done the same joke before, but it's still funny and he still gets into trouble.

Mum's in a mood when she collects Jody and me from school. You always know when adults are upset because they start doing weird things. Mum keeps listening to smoochy music and crying when it's on the radio. When adults get all soppy it's really annoying, isn't it? Whenever I see her upset I ask her why, but she always gives me the same answer. "There's nothing wrong," she says. "I just have something in my eye." But how can she have something in her eye all day?

Mum's playing smoochy music in the car when she turns up at school. It's really loud and I can hear it from the other side of the playground when she parks on the road outside school. She doesn't stop to talk to

28

anyone. She just walks in a straight line across the playground fast, and almost knocking people over as she goes. It looks quite funny. She walks so fast it's like she's on wheels and someone has pushed her across from the car. "Where's Dad?" Jody asks as soon as Mum arrives at the classroom door. Mum takes no notice.

"Where's Dad?" I ask, but just as Mum is about to reply, Grumpy comes over.

"Is everything okay?" Grumpy asks.

Mum looks annoyed, but she says politely, "Everything is fine, thank you."

Grumpy seems to hang around for ages, but when she finally goes away Mum knows what I'm going to ask. "I told you, he's on a secret mission," Mum says angrily, before I get a chance to say anything.

"What sort of secret mission?" Jody and I both ask.

"Just give me a chance to get the car moving. We can talk about it more when we get home."

Mum drives fast and I imagine I am in the back of a racing car. "James Orchard is coming up fast round the bend," the race commentator says in my head. "Orchard is really putting his foot down now. I think he is going to win. He's beating his rival, nasty Nigel. That will show Nigel who's boss. Orchard just cannot be beaten."

When we get home, Jody disappears into the garden and I run straight up to my bedroom. "And James Orchard has won again," the commentator in my head says. "What are your plans now?" he asks. "You've beaten everyone. What

CHAPTER 3
Secrets

Mum always seems to be rushing us through everything since Dad went away. It's as if she doesn't want to spend any time playing with us. She has just rushed us both through our tea again and sent us up to our bedrooms to go to sleep. And it's only seven o'clock! Jody and I just know we won't be able to sleep.

I creep into Jody's bedroom to talk.

"What can we do to get Mum to

tell us what's going on?" Jody asks. "What about if we pretend we are doing a class project on what our dads do and if we don't tell the truth we will get expelled from school," she says.

"No," I reply. "I used that one last week to get extra money to buy chocolate on the way to school. I told Mum we were doing a project on what's in chocolate bars."

At first, Mum doesn't notice that we're talking. We can hear her on the phone downstairs for ages, but she can't hear us. Then, without warning, the thud, thud of her angry footsteps comes up the stairs. She's heard us and now I've got to try to get back to my room without being seen. I creep quickly down the hall and then …

"WHAT ARE YOU DOING?"

It's Mum, she's very angry and

she's shouting. "You should be in bed asleep," she roars. "You've been up here for nearly an hour and I suppose you've woken up your sister."

"No, I … "

"Don't muck around," Mum says. "Just get to bed. I don't want to hear another word."

Just then, Jody looks round the door of her bedroom. "But we can't sleep," she says, and starts to cry. "We want to know where Dad is and we aren't going to go to bed until you tell us." Sometimes Jody can be very brave. I couldn't have done that.

"Oh, I'm sorry," Mum says, looking upset and guilty. Brilliant. Jody's act has worked. Mum now feels so guilty we might actually start to find out what's going on.

"Come here," Mum says, holding

her arms out to both Jody and me. We all have a cuddle and then she asks us to wait at the top of the stairs.

A few seconds later Mum comes back with a newspaper in her hand. Oh no, she's not going to start reading us the boring old news, is she? The paper is all folded up and there's a bit in the middle with a red circle round it.

"You see this newspaper article, the one I've circled?" asks Mum, holding up the paper and pointing at it. Sometimes she asks such silly questions. Of course we can see it.

"Yes," Jody and I say together.

"Well, it's all about where your Dad is."

"Let's see," I say, and I grab the paper from her hands. On it there are some big words saying: "Astronauts Start Mission To Mars."

Underneath, smaller words say: "Three astronauts began humanity's journey to Mars yesterday with a secret launch of the Space Shuttle in America." Then there's a whole load of stuff about presidents and prime ministers.

"What does it say, what does it say?" Jody shouts.

"So where is Dad?" I ask Mum.

"Space," Mum replies.

"Space?" Jody asks.

"Yes," Mum says. "He's working there helping the astronauts who are going to travel to Mars get ready, but it is all very dangerous and no one knows what problems they might find, so the government decided they should keep the trip a secret. That's why even this newspaper doesn't tell anyone who the astronauts are. So you mustn't tell anyone else. Do you understand?"

"Wow," Jody says.

"I don't believe you," I say.

"Well, where do you think he is?" Mum says. "What do you think this newspaper article is about?"

"Really?" I ask, still not quite sure.

"Yes, really," Mum smiles. I suppose she must be telling the truth. It explains why Dad is always playing space games with Jody and me. And that must be why one of the policemen at our house was talking about a "big operation".

"Can we tell our best friends?" I ask.

"No," Mum replies.

"Oh please," Jody says.

"No."

Now I'm annoyed. Mum's kept this secret from us all this time and now she's finally told us, we can't talk to anyone about it.

"Well, why couldn't you just tell

us about Dad's space trip in the first place?" I shout, and run off up to my bedroom.

It is just getting dark and the noise from the nest is getting quieter. A bird is standing on a small twig next to the nest, twisting its head round to poke its beak into its feathers. It's either the mum or the dad, I don't know which.

Isn't it amazing how birds can stand on thin twigs and wires without falling off and at the same time they can twist their heads almost all the way round? Why doesn't it strangle them or make their heads drop off? You would have thought it would make them get crossed wires between their brains and their bodies and that all their wings and legs would get confused about what is supposed to be doing what. Birds are cool.

It would be even more cool if I could twist my head round like a bird's. I'd be able to twist it round in class to see out of the window, look round the class or see someone else's answers without moving. Miss Tadey would never be able to catch me doing it. Mr Stinkin probably would, though. He seems to be able to see anything naughty I do even if it's really small.

As I watch the bird from my bedroom window, it jumps off the twig and flies up to the top of a tree. The chicks can only sit and watch. Flying is fantastic. And blasting off in Dad's spaceship is fantastic too. I know, because I can fly like a bird or a spaceship if I close my eyes and use my power to imagine what I want. You see, Mum isn't the only person keeping secrets. I'm keeping a massive secret. In fact, I'm keeping a planet-size secret. If I think really hard, I can be in Dad's space shuttle or anywhere I want within a few seconds. Jody is the only person I've told about this special power and she doesn't believe me. She says it's all in my head.

Whatever Jody or Mr Stinkin say about me being a dreamer, I know my special power is real. Do they really think I'm just going to sit around waiting for Dad to come home? No way. I am soon sitting next to Dad in his spaceship.

"Ten, nine, eight, seven, six, five, four, three, two, one. We have lift off," the head of the base station says.

"Have you got everything under control?" Dad says to me.

"Yes, I'm fully prepared for our mission," I say. "Where was the last sighting of the evil Detscreacher ship?"

"In Sector 10B – the destruction zone," he says.

We whizz past thousands of stars as we rocket to the speed of light, heading towards the edge of the galaxy. From the small porthole in the side of the ship we see everything blur into weird colours – exploding yellows, reds, greens and a funny purple.

"Do you think we'll complete the mission?" I ask Dad.

"Son, I have every confidence in your secret power," he says.

When we get to Sector 10B, the plan is that I'll fly out of the spaceship hatch and stick a bomb onto the Detscreacher ship.

Dad and I are always having to deal with the Detscreachers. Just two weeks ago, when we came home from swimming, we had to tackle two of them in the kitchen. They were trying to turn our oven into a deadly ray-gun machine.

"Watch out!" shouted Dad, as we got home. "Over by the cooker, are two Detscreachers. Dive for cover."

We all jumped into the corner of the room behind the fridge and Jody and I had to creep over to deactivate the invaders while they weren't looking.

Mum and Dad chose us to deactivate the Detscreachers because we're small and we could get across the room and under the kitchen table without being seen.

"Well done special agents Jody and James," said Mum.

"You will now be remembered throughout history and rewarded with a special banquet," Dad told us. We knew the special banquet would be fish and chips from the shop up the road. It always is and it is always the best.

Now Dad and I have to destroy the terrifying Detscreacher mothership before it attacks Earth. As we slow down to enter Sector 10B, a small fighter mothership protector flashes in front of us and fires one of its thunderbolt stun blasts at us. Dad just pulls us out of the way in time, but some of the thunderbolt hits the back of our ship. The whole tail of the ship is crushed and our air is slowly being sucked out, but Dad still manages to pull the ship round, launch one of our lasers and zap the fighter out of existence.

We don't have much time before our air runs out, but we must complete our mission to destroy the Detscreacher mothership. If we fail, it will destroy our planet.

After a few minutes, in the distance we see the great blue hulk of the mothership, all covered in spikes like some giant hedgehog. It's time for me to use my special powers and head out into space. I've been training for this moment for years and it doesn't take me long to sneak past the ship's defences and fix the bomb underneath. As I fly back to Dad, the black of space turns bright pink as the mothership explodes into dust.

Dad and I must now get back to Earth at full speed while we still have air, but just as we are about to enter Earth's atmosphere a girl's voice begins calling out from the back of the ship. Dad and I try to ignore it. We are concentrating hard on making sure the ship gets back to land safely. Anyone who knows anything about space travel will

46

know how difficult it is to fly a ship into the Earth's atmosphere. If you come in too steep you burn up like a sausage on a barbecue and if you are not steep enough you bounce off the atmosphere like a ball bouncing off a car roof. So, we REALLY need to concentrate. But how can we with a girl calling out all the time?

"Jimmy, Jimmy," she says. "Come here quickly."

I stay with Dad just long enough for us to land safely, and then run to find the girl in the back of the ship. Well, I run to the back of our house, actually. Jody is the girl calling and she's in Mum and Dad's room holding a letter.

"Look what I found," she says. "It was in the washing basket."

"What is it?" I ask.

"A letter."

"I can see that, but what does it

say?"

"It says 'David Orchard is now with us', but someone's torn the rest of it off."

"Great," I say. "Well who's it from, then? Give it to me."

"No. I found it," Jody says. She runs out of the room and locks herself in the toilet. Sisters can be so annoying.

"Come on, Jody," I say. "Don't be silly."

"No. It's mine."

Right, there's nothing else I can do. This is serious. "I've got your teddy," I say.

"Leave it, leave it!"

"Only if you come out and show me the letter."

The door of the toilet opens slowly. "Okay, but don't take it away," Jody says, as she gives me the letter. "Where's my teddy?"

"I don't really have it," I say. "I just said that to get the letter."

"That's mean!" Jody moans.

"Forget it," I say, and we look at the piece of torn, screwed-up paper. The letters HMP are printed at the top of it and then most of the rest of it has been ripped away. The only other words we can see are, "David Orchard is now with us," and an address in Hampshire, England.

"What does it mean?" Jody asks.

"I'll tell you what it means," I say. "It means Mum was lying. That newspaper said the Space Shuttle took off from America, but this letter says Dad is with someone who is in England. Dad's not in space at all. He's somewhere else."

CHAPTER 4
A mystery trip

Mum is behaving more and more strangely all the time. Just the other day she disappeared from the house and left Jody and me on our own. She was probably gone only a few minutes, but it seemed like ages. It was really weird because we could see her at the end of the road sitting on a wall talking on her mobile phone. I don't know why she did that when there was nothing wrong with the phone in the house. And it was raining.

Jody and I have had to be very careful about picking the right time to ask Mum about the letter we found in the washing basket. We try her a few times, but she's in a bad mood and won't tell us anything. Then, for the first time in ages, she actually seems happy. She's talking to us about what we'd like to do at the weekend.

"Mum, what does HMP mean?" I ask.

"Why?" Mum says.

"I'm just interested," I lie.

"Why the sudden interest?"

"We found a letter," Jody blurts out.

"Oh Jody," I shout. "Why couldn't you keep quiet about it?"

"What letter?" Mum asks.

"I found a letter in the washing basket in your room," Jody says. "It says something about Dad being with someone and … "

"… and, look, HMP is printed at the top," I say, pulling the crumpled piece of paper from my pocket. "It comes from somewhere in England and not America, where the Space Shuttle was launched."

Mum's face goes white and then it begins to turn red. Isn't it funny when adults don't know what to say. It doesn't happen often, so when it does it's weird to watch, even if you are upset. Sometimes I play a game with Mum and Dad, asking them questions I know they can't answer. "How many atoms have we got in our bodies?" I asked Dad the other day. He bungled around trying to answer and talked rubbish for ages, before he changed the subject. It was so funny. The best questions to always get both Mum and Dad, though, are the ones about dying and how babies are born. "What happens to us when we die?" or, "How does a baby get in its mum's tummy?" Parents really can give some silly answers. Now Mum can't think of what to say about the letter, but I hope she is not going to get angry.

"Look, I don't know how to tell you this," Mum begins, looking worried. "I'm sorry. I mean ... Well ... It's ... "

"I need the toilet," Jody butts in.

"Oh Jody, can't you wait?" I say.

"No."

"Well, go then," Mum says.

Mum and I sit in silence looking at each other and then she holds her arm out for me to go and have a cuddle. When Jody comes back Mum puts her arms round both of us, we all sit on the floor and she starts again, "Well I didn't tell you the whole truth, but there is a good reason for that."

"Such as?" I say angrily.

"Don't get all cross about it," Mum says. "I did partly tell you the truth, because Dad is on a top secret mission. But I couldn't tell you all the truth because then I would have been in trouble with the government."

"So what does HMP mean and what is Dad doing?" I ask, getting more annoyed.

"HMP means Her Majesty's Person. The letter comes from the head of the Royal Navy. Your Dad is a captain in the Royal Navy and he is on a very, very important mission at sea. He … "

"Why doesn't the letter come from a ship, then?" Jody interrupts. Good question, Jody. Don't let Mum get away with telling us silly stories.

"Well, the Royal Navy has to have offices somewhere," Mum explains.

"Why did you lie to us?" Jody whines.

"Because what he does for the Royal Navy is really cloak and dagger stuff," Mum says.

"Cloak and what?" I snap back. What is Mum talking about?

"Sorry. Cloak and dagger means that what he is doing has to be kept really private. No one must know about it. Just wait there a minute."

Mum disappears to the other end of the house and comes back with a newspaper. Not again! She shows Jody and me an article about lots of ships doing something important and then looks very pleased with herself. "You see, that's where Dad is and it is important enough to be in the newspaper."

"That's what you said last time when you showed us the newspaper and you lied to us about him going into space," I complain.

"Well, you'll just have to believe me now," Mum orders. She looks like she's just about had enough of our questions. "I promise it's the truth."

I suppose Mum has a point. There's not much Jody and I can do. And what she says does make sense. Dad is brave, after all. I remember the time he climbed on next door's roof to rescue their cat. I know Dad frightened it up there by catching it with the hose spray when we were having a water fight, but it was still cool to see him climb up to the rescue. Watching him bounce up the ladder in his wet shorts made us all laugh.

There was also the time he

accidentally set fire to the garden fence by putting too many dry leaves on the bonfire and building it too close to the fence. But he was brave for going near to it to put it out before it did much damage. Mum had a real go at him, but she didn't really mean it. She thought it was funny and so did we.

I wander back to my bedroom and all the birds in the nest seem to be sitting still. Maybe they are also thinking about being heroes. They'll have to be very brave when they try to fly for the first time and Dad's mission sounds like it's just as daring. He might not be able to survive without my help, so I decide to use my special power to get to his ship. I lie on my bed, close my eyes, and quickly begin to fly up into the sky.

The clouds blacken and the sky

gets as dark as the worst night in *Lord of the Rings*. Rain is pouring on to the grey, cold sea and the waves are so high they look like rocky mountains. Two pirate ships have trapped HMS Boldsail, my Dad's ship, and lots of horrible men are crawling all over it. I land on the deck and two pirates try to push me overboard. Dad must be in real trouble.

I use my special-power ray gun to blast them to bits and start looking for Dad. Below deck everyone is fighting and some of the cabins are on fire.

"You cannot win," says a loud voice. "Give up! The Pompmouth Pirates have you surrounded. There is no escape."

There's no escape? Who do they think they are? They obviously do not know who my Dad is. If they did, they would never have had the guts to attack his ship in the first place. As I get further and further into the body of the ship, the electricity is beginning fail. The lights are flickering on and off and the smell of smoke from the fires would stop any normal person breathing. Of course, I am no normal person, so I can breathe even in the most horrible air.

Just as I am about to give up hope of finding Dad, I hear a voice echoing from deep inside a gloomy, airless hall. "J," I am sure it calls. "Jimmy." There it is again. "J." I recognise that voice. It's Dad! As I begin trying to work out how I will get to him when I can't even see him, a pirate with a gun jumps out from the doorway.

"Put your hands up," he shouts.

I aim my ray gun to stop him, but it won't work. I must have used up all its power, firing at pirates on the way down. I quickly put my hands up and the pirate grabs me from behind.

"J," I can hear Dad's voice shout. "Jimmy, are you alright?"

Before I can answer, the pirate is dragging me off back to the deck.

As we get towards the deck, we start to climb a steep ladder and I see my chance to escape. I kick the pirate down and he drops his gun under some big boxes. He tries to get it back, but he cannot reach it. Now he's really angry. He races back to the ladder and begins climbing up behind me, shouting and pulling a massive knife from the back of his trousers. As I reach the deck above, he grabs my foot and tugs me back. I keep trying my ray gun, but it won't work. I kick back at him like a crazy horse and he just keeps climbing up

and up, pulling me back. I know that, unless I can get rid of him, Dad and I will be finished.

As he slides onto the deck behind me I muster all the strength I can and kick him backwards. Just as I've had enough and I'm about to give up, I see blood trickling down the side of his face. He has banged his head on a big metal tap and is dazed, but he has just enough energy to plunge at me with his knife. I dodge out of the way as he staggers to the floor unconscious. I run back towards the place where Dad's voice is coming from. At last, I find him, untie his hands and release him.

"Thanks, mate. You were amazing," he says, hugging me and showing me a hidden passage for us to get out to a lifeboat.

When we get to the lifeboat it is surrounded by pirates, so we hide in a doorway and …

"I'm, here," a voice shouts. "Come and say hello to your Nan."

It's a voice from back at our house, but I can't go and leave Dad struggling like this. I must finish the mission.

"You take the two on the right and I'll take the two on the left," Dad says.

We jump out from doorway and attack The Pompmouth Pirates with all our strength. Within minutes, they are all lying dazed on the deck and Dad and I rush towards the lifeboat. As we start to untie it, the pirates begin getting up. It looks like they are going to capture us and all the time I am being distracted by that voice from back at our house.

"I can't go, I must stay and help Dad," I keep muttering.

We just manage to push the

lifeboat into the water and jump into it while the pirates are making one last grab to pull us back. They keep shooting at us as we row as fast as we can to a nearby Royal Navy ship. Luckily, Pompmouth Pirates don't have a very good aim.

Mission accomplished. Now I can head back home.

Downstairs, Nan has just arrived. "Oh look, hasn't he grown," she says to Mum. Nan brushes my hair with her hand as she talks.

I can't have grown that much since last time she saw me. It was only last week. "Nan is going to look after you for the day while I go out," Mum says.

"Great," Jody and I shout together. Nan always gives us lots of treats.

"Where are you going?" Jody asks.

"Out," Mum says.

"Where?" Jody says.

"Just out. It's really important."

It is strange that Mum has something so important to do that she has to disappear for a whole day. She's not said anything about it before.

"But ... ," I say, before Nan interrupts me.

"Your Mum has got important things to do and she has to get off," Nan says. "Don't drive her mad. I've got lots of fun things planned. Give Mum a kiss and go and play while I make myself a cup of tea. "

While Nan is drinking her tea, Jody and I do a bit more searching in the bedrooms upstairs to see if we can find out any more about Dad's mission on the ship. We can't stop talking about Mum's strange behaviour and it has made us very suspicious. I have another look in the drawer at the bottom of Mum and Dad's wardrobe, where I know they keep lots of important things. Yesterday the drawer was empty, which was curious. Now, it is full up again. So full, in fact, I can only just about open it. I wish I hadn't. There, right on the top is a photograph taken when we were all on a boat trip on holiday last year. And there, at the side of the boat, Dad is being sick.

I call Jody in to have a look.

"Can you see what I can see?" I ask.

"What?"

"Dad is being sick. Dad is always sick when we go on a boat, even on a rowing boat on the lake in the park."

"So?"

"So that means he can't be a sailor.

It means Mum has told us yet another pretend story about Dad!"

CHAPTER 5
From Brazil to Burpy Brad

Sometimes finding out the truth can be tough. But it can also be better to know the truth, even though it may be hard, than to spend every day wondering what is going on, your head filling with question after question. If we can't believe Mum, who can we believe? What sort of game is Mum playing, keeping the truth from us? Does she think we are stupid?

It is Friday and I am thinking about Mum as I watch the rain dribble down the windows during a lesson in Mr Stinkin's class. He seems to be waffling on about something to do with multiplication. I'm having bets with myself about which rain drop will reach the bottom of the window first.

"Is the answer out of the window?" Stinkin shouts.

Oh no, he can see I'm not taking any notice of his lesson.

"I was just thinking about the best way to do your sums," I lie. And then a miracle happens. Before Stinkin gets a chance to give me his usual angry treatment, Grumpy storms through the classroom door.

"Mr Stunkin, what are you doing in here?" Grumpy asks, marching across the room. "You are supposed to be in ... "

Before she can say any more she trips on Stinkin's bag and a small dog crawls out. Everyone in the class is rolling around laughing. There is no way Stinkin will be telling me off for dreaming in class today.

"Mr Stunkin, what on Earth is this?" Grumpy screams.

"It's a ... It's a ... "

"It's a dog, I can see that, but what is it doing here? Pets are not allowed in school and they should certainly not be kept in your bag!"

"His name's Crusher, he's not an it," Stinkin moans.

"Crusher! What sort of name is that for a tiny dog like that?" Grumpy sneers.

"Well, it's ... "

"I don't care. Please come to my office straight away. Miss Tadey will be taking over the class for the rest of the day."

As Grumpy says this, a very confused-looking Toady walks through the door behind her. "A dog called Crusher," Toady says, grinning and looking back at a very embarrassed Stinkin.

At least the rest of the day can only get better. Anyway, there's only an hour to go before we go home.

Mum is still away on her day out and Nan comes to collect us. When we get home, Nan tries to get us to play some games, but since we found the photograph of Dad throwing up on a rowing boat, we can't think about anything else. As soon as Mum comes through the front door, I run at her with the picture.

"What's this?" I shout.

"A photograph," Mum says.

"I know it's a photograph, but

look at Dad," I say.

"What about him?"

"He's … "

Before I can get the rest of my words out, my sister interrupts. "He's being sick, which means he can't be a sailor," she says. "So what is he really doing?"

There she goes again. Straight in with the killer question. How does she do it?

"Now, now," Nan says, as she rushes to the front door. "Give your Mum a chance to get in. What's all the fuss?"

What's all the fuss? WHAT'S ALL THE FUSS? Our Dad has gone missing, Mum keeps telling us lies and Nan asks what all the fuss is? Before Mum has a chance to think, I begin to cry. I don't know why. It just starts to happen. "What's the big secret?" I scream. "He's my Dad and

I want to know where he is."

"He's my Dad too and I also want to know where he is," Jody says, a bit confused by all the shouting.

Mum kneels down, puts her arm round me and tells me not to worry. "There's nothing wrong with having a good cry," she says.

That's what adults always say when children cry. I hate crying. I always feel so silly, but I do feel better afterwards. I am still angry with Mum for not telling me and Jody the truth. If she thinks a quick cuddle will sort things out, she's going to have a big surprise. "Well, what is the big secret and where is Dad," I say, pushing her away.

Mum stands up and walks over to kiss Jody, who turns away. "Look, I've said all I can say," Mum whispers.

Why she is whispering, I don't

know.

"I'm tired of having to explain myself all the time," Mum mutters, as she goes to the kitchen.

"You two need to be nice to your Mum," Nan says. "She's a bit upset at the moment."

Well we know that, but we want to know why.

"I'm going to be staying for a few days, to help out. Won't that be fun", Nan says, trying to change the subject.

Later in the day, Jody and I give Mum the silent treatment when she asks us to do our homework. Why should we help her when she won't help us? We expect her to get annoyed, but it is really weird because she just walks out of the room and says nothing. A few minutes later, Nan comes in.

"Doing your homework is to help

you, not your Mum," she says.

"Yeah, yeah, yeah," I say. I'm angry enough to get back at Nan with much worse replies, but I hold back, because she is Nan, after all. She's different. I have a whole store of special words and curses I can launch if I want to have a go at Mum or Dad. "Slug head," is a good one. But I might also use "chicken brain", "bum features", or "camel breath". Also, saying anything with "poo" in it is very satisfying and always winds adults up. "Go and poo yourself," is a good curse. I've got loads of other words that are even worse. You know how you have some really special rude words for using when you badly want to bug an adult.

I have held back with Nan, but she is still annoyed.

"Don't get sarcastic with me,

young man," she snaps back.

I've never seen her angry before and she's never called me "young man" before either. She sits down beside Jody and me and starts to talk, really gently.

"There is a very good reason why Mum has not told you the truth," she says sitting on the sofa and putting her arms round both of us. "She's trying to protect you. She doesn't want me to tell you this, so you'll have to keep it quiet, but your Dad is … well no, I better not tell you."

"You must!" Jody and I scream.

"Hush," Nan whispers. 'We don't want Mum to hear. I'll tell you only if you promise to keep it really quiet."

"We will."

"All right. I hope Mum doesn't find out I've told you. If you really want to know."

"Yes."

"Your Dad is a spy." As Nan tells us more, she looks at the door to the room, nervously. "Tell me if you see Mum and we'll have to quickly change the subject."

"OK."

"Have you heard of a country called Brazil?"

"Yes. That's where Ronaldo comes from."

"Who?"

"Ronaldo, the best footballer in the world."

"Oh really. Well, your Dad's the best Dad in the world and he's on a secret mission."

"You're sounding like Mum," I say. "How can we believe you?"

"I'm your Nan, aren't I. I don't play the silly games parents play."

"Well, what about the letter with

HMP on it?" I ask. "What does that mean?"

"It means your Dad is Her Majesty's Person, but it is from the head of the secret service." Nan explains. "It couldn't say any more than that, could it, because it's all secret?"

"So what's he doing in Brazil?" I ask.

"You mean Brazil," Nan says.

"I said Brazil," I say. Nan sometimes has a bit of trouble hearing.

"Oh, I don't know. Even your Mum doesn't know the details, but we do know that he's on a dangerous operation. We worried about telling you, because if enemy spies find out that you know... "

"What would they do?" Jody asks, looking worried.

"They might tickle you all over to

get at the truth," Nan jokes, starting to tickle us both.

"You mean they might torture us to tell them what they want," I say. "I've seen it on a James Bond film and on *Spy Kids*. If you were so worried about us getting into trouble, why are you telling us now?"

"Because I could see you really wanted to find out about your Dad and I think you are both old enough to know the truth. You are certainly old enough to keep a secret. You will keep it secret won't you?" Nan says seriously.

"Yes," Jody and I say.

"Good," Nan says. "Now do your homework."

I tell Nan I am going to my room to do my homework, but really I want to look at the bird's nest. The chicken-leg chicks are getting bigger, but they still don't move from the nest. They can't fly yet and they keep getting food brought to them by their mum, or perhaps it's their dad. I wonder what my dad's doing now? Is he fighting off some evil spies or breaking into a top-secret research station on Brazil? He's probably waiting for my help.

I lie on my bed, close my eyes and soon I'm soaring out over the rooftops. In no time at all, I'm flying over the Atlantic Ocean. I can see boats, like tiny toys, bobbing around in the water below me. It's just getting dark when I leave home, but as I fly I follow the sun, and full daylight returns after a few minutes. Dad told me that the further west you go the later night-time arrives, because the sun rises in the east and sets in the west. Wouldn't it be great to be so far west that the sun never set? Although, I suppose if you keep going too long, you go right round the world and end up back where you started. Anyway, using my special powers means I can fly thousands of miles an hour to catch up with the sun.

I use my powers of detection to find Dad in Brazil, but what I see doesn't look good. He is imprisoned in a big castle, like the Tower of London, which looks strange next to lots of sandy beaches and palm trees. I land quietly near a window and see Dad, strapped to a chair in a cave-like room filled with gadgets. An old man in a white coat and glasses is standing over him, threatening him.

"So, Mr Orchard, who sent you?" the white-coated man says. I'm sure I've seen him before somewhere. Yes, he looks like Grumpy dressed as a man. Perhaps he's Grumpy's brother? Now that IS frightening!

"Whatever you do to me, I won't tell you," Dad says.

"If you are not going to help me, why shouldn't I end our little friendship now, forever?"

"If you kill me, my people will send other agents and then more. You won't get away with your plan."

"But it is such a sweet plan, don't you think?" the old man says, as he moves a huge machine that looks a bit like a rubber satellite dish with a boxing glove stuck on the end. "No other scientist could have invented this. When people called me an egghead at school because I thought up my own scientific experiments, I was planning for this moment. I always knew I would do better than that clever-clogs Ian Kat." And he started to laugh hysterically, like a madman.

83

The scientist stops, looks embarrassed and clears his throat. "Egh, eghm. As I was saying, my plan is beautifully simple," he says, patting the rubber satellite-dish thing as he speaks. "I'll focus this amazing machine, the movemutator, on the footballers of Brazil. They have more energy than anyone else in the world and my machine will suck it all out. Just think how powerful it will make me. And I'm starting with the most energetic of all the Brazilian players, the crazy footballers on Copacabana Beach in Rio. Just think of all that energy wasted on silly soccer moves – slide tackles, scissor-kicks and backsides."

"I think you mean back-heels," Dad interrupts.

"You are in no position to argue," the scientist says.

"Aghh, the famous back-heel trick

of kicking the ball with the heel, perfected by Brazil's Socrates years ago," Dad adds, keeping his cool brilliantly. "I remember…"

"Shutup!" the scientist shouts. "I'll suck the energy from all the footballers, then turn my machine on the Brazilian dancers at one of their famous carnivals. My movemutator will enable me to make everyone in any city shake madly. They'll have to give me whatever I want or face an eternity of frightening football and diabolical dance, with people wobbling around all over the place like gigantic jellies. I'll rule the world. Everyone will have to play my game." He bursts into a chilling laugh again that sounds like the noise of an angry chimpanzee.

"I don't get the joke," Dad says. He's starting to look nervous and I realise I have to release him. I throw a rock through an open window in a nearby room and the scientist rushes out of sight to see what the noise is. I jump in, untie Dad and fly him out of the window as the scientist comes back into the room.

"Fools, you'll never escape," the scientist shouts.

"Thanks son. You've saved me again," Dad says, as we speed off. Suddenly he shouts, "Watch out!" as we narrowly miss a tree.

"That was close," I say, managing to dodge past the top of a tall flag-pole.

"It's not over yet," Dad says. "We must stop Smith's attack at the Copacabana Beach."

"Smith. Who's Smith?" I ask.

"He's that mad scientist back at the castle."

"And he's called Smith, not

something more frightening like Dr Laser, Goldcannon or Smirski?"

"You've watched too many James Bond films," Dad says, as we land at the Copacabana Beach. Masked dancers in fantastic feathered outfits and people blowing whistles or banging drums swirl all around us, and fun football matches are being played all over the beach. "Of course, it's carnival time," Dad says. "That's why Smith chose now to start his plan. He carries the movemutator on his van. Look out for it. He's so full of himself its got his name on the side."

After searching for the van for what seems like ages we see it near to a football match on the beach. We rush over to it and Dad whispers: "Ok, I know it's risky son, but you are going to have to do your stuff." I wriggle underneath the van, swap the wires to the movemutator and slide out.

As fireworks blast off from every rooftop, the music gets louder and the footballers and dancers get more frantic. Suddenly, Smith falls out from the back of his van. My plan of swapping the wires must have worked. Smith must have tried to zap the footballers, and the movemutator must have back-fired on him. Like huge ice creams, Smith and his van melt away, leaving only his glasses and white coat on the ground.

"Thanks to you, Smith has been stopped and the world is a safer place," Dad says. "Well done, son."

It's time for me to fly home and I must leave Dad to sort out everything with his other agents. It's a long journey back.

The next day, as usual, I wake up

to the sound of the birds outside my bedroom window. I sit in bed watching them, they all seem a bit excited. Then, suddenly, one of the chicks leaps from the nest and, just as it looks like it is going to crash to the ground, it flies. It's the first time I've seen any of the chicks leave the nest. "Come here quickly Jody, Mum, Dad," I call. Then I remember Dad's not here.

Mum and Jody run in, wondering what's wrong. "They're flying," I say, pointing at the nest. Mum begins to cry. I don't know why. "Something in my eye," she lies. "The birds have really changed. Just think how brave they must be to fly for the first time, not knowing if they can do it."

While Mum is here I decide to make sure she doesn't know Nan has told us about Dad spying. "I bet

Dad's being brave on his mission on the ship," I say.

"As brave as those little birds," she replies.

After seeing the chick fly, I can't wait to get to school. I know that everything is going to change now and get better for me as well. I want to tell all my friends about the birds and the even more exciting news about Dad being a spy. I know Nan said I mustn't, but you know about adult secrets. If they are juicy, you've just got to tell your friends.

I tell Ahmed about Dad first and I'm not sure he believes me. He seems more convinced when I tell some of the other people in my class and then everyone is really impressed. I wonder how many of their dads can be as important and as brave as mine?

I am feeling happy for the first

time in ages when, at the end of school, a strange and annoying thing happens. Burpy Brad, a horrible boy from the year above mine, shouts at me across the playground. "Your Dad's not a spy," he laughs, smiling round at his group of friends. "We know where he is and he's certainly not in Brazil."

Before I get a chance to teach that slug-head of a boy a lesson and find out what he means, he's jumped on the bus and is gone. I know he's always ruining everyone's fun and I should ignore him, but what he says keeps spinning round and round in my mind. What was he talking about? Is he just being horrible or does he really know something I don't? And if he does, is Mum going mad? Perhaps Mum and Nan really don't know the truth.

CHAPTER 6
The truth

When I thought Mum was not telling me the truth I felt lonely, like she no longer cared about me. Now I am suspicious of what Nan told Jody and me and I feel worse. All I want to know, more than anything else, is the truth and now the only person who seems to want to tell me the truth is the person I hate the most – Burpy Brad. And he wants to do it only so he can make fun of me.

That night, I can't sleep for

thinking about what Burpy Brad said about my Dad's mission in Brazil. I haven't told Jody and I daren't tell Mum. I feel I can't talk about it to anyone and I can't wait to get to school in the morning to find out what bum features was talking about. I wake up really early and I'm dressed before Mum gets to my room to get me up. She is really surprised.

"Wow, look at you," she says. "Can you really be my son, up before me in the morning?"

Don't you hate it when adults try to be sarcastic, especially first thing in the morning.

"Come down for breakfast," Mum says.

"I'm not hungry," I say.

"I'll eat his," Jody says. "I'm starving."

"You've got to eat, Jimmy," Mum

tells me. "You'll be hungry when you get to school. And you don't want to end up having to eat mini-beasts, spiders and ants, in the playground," she laughs. I laugh, a little bit. It is quite funny and for a minute I forget about Dad.

"I could, of course, make you some mini-beast sandwiches now, if you want," Mum says. "How about squashed worm and tomato ketchup or fly surprise or there's the house speciality, roast slug and mustard."

"Oh, Rachel, don't be so disgusting," Nan says to Mum, as she comes into the kitchen, still in her dressing gown. "You'll upset the children."

Jody and I are really laughing now. When adults have a go at each other for being disgusting, it is really funny.

All of us – Mum, Nan, Jody and I

– are laughing now. Burpy Brad seems a million miles away. Then I see the picture on the fridge of Mum, Dad, Jody and me at the funfair, when we were splashing into the water on the big dipper. Suddenly I feel guilty for laughing and having fun when I don't know where Dad is. Everyone else is still in stitches and that only makes me feel worse.

"It's not funny," I shout.

"All right, mister serious," Mum says, as everyone goes quiet. "Anyway, it's time for school. Clean your teeth and come straight back downstairs."

When we come back down, Nan kisses us all goodbye and Mum walks us to school. She takes us to our classrooms and gives us a hug just in time for the register, which is really annoying because it means I won't be able to speak to Burpy until break time.

Lessons before the break seem to take ages and they usually seem faster than afternoon lessons. But today starts off with the time going really slowly so by this afternoon, time will have nearly stopped. Imagine that! Imagine if you really could stop time and then travel through it. Then I could go back to when Dad was still at home and ask him where he was going to go.

Time is really dragging, as Mr Stinkin teaches us about maths, but I know that once I get hold of Burpy everything will be different.

After a long wait, playtime arrives. I rush outside and can see Burpy standing on the other side of the playground. As I walk towards him he sees me and starts laughing. He holds up a newspaper and starts shouting, repeating himself over and over. "We know where your Dad is and he's not in Brazil. We know where your Dad is and he's not in Brazil."

I begin to run and I am quickly standing in front of Burpy. He goes quiet and his friends all stare at me. What can I do now? I want to hit him, but then he may never tell me about Dad. We stand and watch each other for what seems like forever. Burpy has a sickening grin on his face.

"Well, what do you want, Orchard?" Burpy steps closer as he speaks.

"What did you mean about my Dad?" I ask.

"Do you read the newspaper?" grins Burpy. "You should do. It's good to know what's going on in the world. It's good for the brain."

"Stop mucking around," I shout.

"What do you know about my Dad?"

Burpy opens the newspaper he has been holding in his hand. He reads, "David Orchard was today sent to prison for one year for his part in the burglary of Jamal's electrical store. He had …"

I grab the paper from Burpy's hands. "Don't snatch," he barks, sarcastically.

David Orchard was today sent to prison for one year for his part in the burglary of Jamal's electrical store. There are the horrible words, ice cold and clear. I feel like the whole world is crushing into my head and my ears are whistling. Can it be true? The paper goes on, *Orchard had claimed he was innocent and then decided to confess last week.*

That can't be my Dad, I think. He's really brave and very

important. Why would he get mixed up in a burglary? Why would anyone want to send him to prison? The words 'burglary' and 'prison' bounce round in my head. I feel dizzy. I hate Burpy! I rush forward throwing my fists around at his face, but he backs away and by the time I get near to him, a teacher is standing next to us. It's Toady.

"What's going on?" Toady is angry.

"Nothing," all of us mumble.

"I can see something is going on."

"We're just playing," I mutter. The last thing I want is a teacher getting involved.

"OK. Be careful." Adults think they are so clever but they can easily be fooled.

"It's all lies," I whisper to Burpy. Toady is still standing quite close by.

"Oh yeah," Burpy blurts out.

"Why would the paper lie about your Dad? You know it's true, but you just don't like it."

He's right. There is nothing worse than someone you hate being right. And to make it worse, he is the only person who has told me the one thing I have been dying to know since Dad went away. I take the paper and walk away on my own. I can hear Burpy and his mates giggling as the bell rings for the end of playtime.

Back in class, I get all the spelling questions wrong and Mr Stinkin keeps telling me off for staring out of the window again. I don't even know I am doing it, but as I think about the newspaper article that's now in my pocket, I keep drifting off into a dream. Mr Stinkin doesn't see Chris and Sarah sitting over by the bookshelf looking at me and pretending they are holding the bars of a prison. I don't want to tell Stinkin or any of the other teachers what's happening, because I don't want them to know where Dad is. So I ignore all the teasing.

Questions keep flying round in my head. Why did Dad do it? Will we still see him? Should I tell Jody? What will she do? Why have Mum and Nan not told us the truth? Then I realise there's a simple answer to the last question, at least. Mum and Nan have kept the truth from Jody and me because they don't know the truth. They wouldn't lie to us if they knew the truth, would they?

Lunchtime is miserable. Burpy and his mates and Chris and Sarah keep teasing me. "Does your Dad like porridge?" they say, or, "Never mind about Harry Potter and the Prisoner of Azkaban, here's Jimmy

Orchard and the Prisoner of Brazil." Everywhere I turn I seem to see their ugly faces grinning, laughing, talking about me. There's nothing I can do. Then I see Jody. I must tell her before Burpy gets to her.

"Why are all those boys laughing at you?" she asks. Jody has already seen that something is wrong. I must tell her quickly, so she knows what is going on. We go back into the school building in the corridor that leads to the toilets, so Burpy and his mates can't interfere, and I tell her the truth.

"Look at this," I tell her, unfolding the newspaper.

"What?"

"This story, here," I point. Jody reads slowly.

"It says Dad's in prison." Jody looks confused.

"I know," I say.

"It's not true."

"It is true. It's the only story that makes sense. Remember the police leaving with Dad early in the morning. He wasn't going on a special mission, he was being arrested."

"So why didn't Mum and Nan tell us then?"

"The answer is obvious."

"Well?"

"They don't know the truth. The problem is that now we know the truth, how will we keep it from them? We don't want to upset them."

"We'll have to pretend we believe what they've told us," Jody says.

"I know, but now Nan thinks we think Dad is in Brazil and Mum still thinks we think he's on a ship."

News about Dad spreads fast round the school and soon children are making fun of Jody as well as me. We both have a horrible day, but when Mum arrives in the car to collect us we pretend we are really happy.

"Any news from Dad's ship?" Jody shouts from the back seat next to me. It's another one of her strokes of genius. Copying my questions at breakfast the other day, of course, but still clever. What better way to get Mum to think we believe her story than to ask her to tell us more.

"I heard that yesterday they practised submarine operations," Mum explains.

"Really," I say. "What do they have to do for that?"

"They spend time on a mini-submarine looking around the ocean."

"Wow!" Jody and I pretend to be impressed.

When we get home, Mum heads upstairs and Nan comes out of the front room to say hello.

"Doesn't your Nan get a kiss?" she says, bending down and shoving her face towards Jody and me. We both kiss her and I ask, "Any news about Dad?"

"Well, of course, there's only a little bit," Nan whispers. "The mission is going well, but it may take a little longer than planned because there are more enemy agents than they expected."

"How much longer?" Jody asks.

"Could be a few months, but he'll stay in touch," Nan says.

"Oh no." Jody and I pretend we are surprised by Nan's news. Then Mum comes back into the room and starts telling us more and more about what Dad is supposed to be doing on his ship. She is clearly pleased Jody and I seem to believe everything she says, but this storytelling could get very confusing. Mum and Nan each think we believe their stories and Mum doesn't know Nan has told us the story about Brazil.

Usually, fooling adults is easy. I once convinced Mum and Dad we'd won the lottery. Dad always buys different numbers and can never remember what they are. We were all watching TV and as the numbers were called I kept saying, "Yes, got it." When we had them all I said, "We seem to have them all, does that mean we've won?" Dad jumped out of his seat and Mum couldn't stop laughing. When they saw we hadn't won, I got the tickle treatment. Mum, Dad and Jody all tickled me until I said each one of them was wonderful.

There was also the time when, first thing one morning, I pretended to Dad that the car was rolling down the hill. He ran outside to stop it, still dressed in only his pants. Mrs Pringle, who was cutting her hedge across the road, was really shocked. Dad went really red and we all thought it was hilarious.

That was then, before Dad disappeared. Or, I suppose, now I should say, "before Dad went to prison". Now everything is different, everything is more confusing. Jody and I don't want to go to school to hear everyone teasing us and making fun of what has happened to Dad. We will have to fool Mum into thinking we are ill, so we can stay at home for the rest of the week. We both say we have tummy aches and when Mum takes our temperatures we play the old trick of warming up the thermometer on our bedside light bulbs.

"You both have a bit of a fever, so you can stay at home," Mum says. "It wouldn't be because you are worried about Dad, would it? Are you OK about him now?"

"Yes, I'm not upset any more," I lie. "I think my tummy hurts because of those chocolates I ate yesterday."

"Me too," Jody says.

Mum does not look completely sure we are telling the truth, but she is convinced enough to let us stay off school for the rest of the week. I know we can't carry on like this forever. We will have to go to school eventually and I have no idea how we will carry on keeping the truth from Mum. Life has been confusing since the police took Dad and it has

just become a thousand times more
complicated.

CHAPTER 7

A run for my life

Today is a bad day, a very bad day. Mum has stopped believing we are ill and she has forced us to go to school. Now Jody and I have to face Burpy Brad and his horrible mates. As we go through the school gates, there he is, grinning away and whispering to his friends. I know what he's saying. But he's not tough enough to say anything to Jody and me until Mum has gone.

"Do you like porridge?" Burpy

shouts across the playground, as he turns to his friends and sniggers. They all find it really funny. Jody takes no notice and disappears into the school building, but I can't ignore it and ... and then it's too much.

"What's your problem," I shout. "Why do you think you are so clever? You are just an idiot who can't think of anything better to do." Burpy's face turns from its usual pink colour to a sort of grey. He looks at me like he is going to throw himself at me and he grabs my shirt. I manage to snatch myself away and make a run for it. No one seems to want to stick up for me and Burpy is too big for me to fight. As I run across the playground, I knock over a little girl. "Sorry," I shout, as I keep running past her. She seems to be all right.

I start running towards the school building, hoping someone will stop Burpy so I can run into the classroom, but everyone just watches, laughs, cheers. As I get to the door, one of Burpy's best friends steps out and into my way. I turn, dodge past Burpy and run back towards the school gate. That football training is useful after all.

Now I'm really worried, getting tired and out of breath. I drop my rucksack, but I daren't stop to pick it up. Burpy Brad will catch me. I speed out of the gate and on to the road, hoping Burpy won't dare to leave school, but he doesn't care. I look back and see Grumpy, Stinkin and Toady chasing Burpy out of the gates. Great, now I'll be in trouble with them for running out of school. I don't know what I can do apart from keep running.

The teachers aren't used to running like this, and dodging round people walking down the street. Toady dashes down the wrong road and we are soon losing the others. Grumpy slips into a flower stall and ends up covered in water and plants. Stinkin bumps into a policewoman and is nearly arrested. It would be really funny, but I'm too scared of Burpy to laugh.

As I'm nearly across the road, a car swerves to avoid running me over. "Sorry," I shout, again. I keep sprinting, going as fast as I can, but Burpy seems stuck to me like some sort of guided missile.

Now I am nearly at the high street. There's the CD shop, playing Kylie Minogue, as usual, and there's the cafe Mum sometimes takes us to. But where's Burpy? As I look back over my shoulder to see where he is, I trip and bump into someone. It's old Elsie, our next door neighbour. "Are you alright love?" she asks.

Of course I'm not alright, but I can't tell her that or she'll tell Mum.

Elsie's a really annoying busybody. She's always telling tales to Mum about Jody and me. Some days it gets really silly. She'll knock on the door or poke her head over the garden fence every ten minutes with some story or other. "Rachel, I don't like to interfere," she always starts saying to Mum. Then she lists the most stupid things. "Did you know Jimmy has been picking grass?" (or "squashing flies" or "breathing"). Mum says it's because she's lonely, but I think she is just a pain.

She's certainly being a pain now. She won't stop questioning me and I keep telling her I'm okay, as I glance back to see where Burpy is. I can see his reflection in the car parked opposite. He's hiding in a shop doorway.

"Are you sure you're alright?" Elsie adds. "Why are you running so fast?"

"I'm late for lessons."

"But you're running the wrong way for school and shouldn't you be with your M...?"

I can't stand still listening to her questions any longer. I can see Burpy slowly making his way up the street and he'll be on my back as soon as Elsie finds someone else to annoy, unless I get moving now. As I run off, Elsie shouts after me, "Are you sure you're . . . ?"

"I'm fine, really, but don't want to be late. See you."

As she turns to carry on walking, Burpy bashes into her in his hurry to catch me. While he is still confused, I run off into the alley next to Bosgood, the toyshop Dad always takes me to – or, now he's no longer here, I should say, the toyshop he used to take me to. I dive into a doorway and watch for Burpy.

After a couple of minutes, he goes running past the end of the alley. He must think I've carried on running up the main road. I breathe the biggest sigh of my life, so big it sounds like a dinosaur breathing, and begin walking back up the alley to get back to school. Then, as I look up to the main road, there's the worst sight ever. It's Burpy and he's looking straight at me.

I quickly turn and run back down the alley, but it doesn't take long before I realise I've made a big mistake. There's no way out at the other end. Burpy will have me trapped. I stop, turn and face him. I have no choice. Surprised, he stops as well.

"What are you going to do now, bone-head?" Burpy shouts. "There's no where to run, is there? But I'm sure your Dad must have told you what that's like. What's the matter? Oh, of course, I forgot, he's a spy isn't he, so he will have told you how to escape from being cornered."

"You think you're so clever making fun of me, don't you?" I say, trying to buy time to think of a way to escape. "Everyone hates you, Burpy, and getting them to laugh at me is the only way you can get their attention, isn't it? It's sad, you're sad." Now I'm really frightened and I'm trying not to cry. He's also nervous, which is why he hasn't beaten me up yet. Perhaps he thinks I'm stronger than I am.

Burpy and I stand shouting at each other for what seems like ages. Then he rushes towards me and just when I think he's going to beat me up, there's a miracle. A voice is shouting at us from the main road.

"What are you doing?" It's the Tomlin Twins, Ben and Becky. They're from year six. They'll be in big school next year. I've only talked with them a few times, but I'm very glad to see them now.

"I said, what are you doing?" Ben snaps. Burpy stops dead like a statue. As he turns towards the twins, he pretends he's been having fun and starts smiling at them.

"We're just having a laugh, aren't we," Burpy says, turning to me with a sick, nasty smile.

"Ye …" Before I can say anything Becky interrupts.

"You were having a go at Jimmy,

weren't you, sicko?" she says.

"No I wasn't," Burpy yells.

"Then why's he looking so upset," she says, as she points at me. "What was he saying to you? Was he having a go at you about your Dad?" "Well …" I don't have a chance to say any more.

"You were having a go about his Dad being in prison, weren't you?" Ben shouts. "Well, shall we tell him about your Dad?"

Now Burpy is looking really worried, but I can't understand why. "No, let's not talk about my Dad," he begs, starting to cry. I almost feel sorry for him. What can be so terrible?

"I think we should talk about your Dad," Ben says. "Do you want to know where Mr Burpy, father of this brave little boy, is, Jimmy?"

"Yes," I whisper. I can only just

get the word out. Everything is so confusing. "Where is he?"

"Why don't you tell him?" Becky says, nodding over towards Burpy.

"Let's leave it now and I promise I won't have a go at Jimmy any more," Burpy moans.

"Now it would be a shame to leave everyone wondering like that, wouldn't it, Burpy?" Becky says.

"It would, wouldn't it?" Ben says, laughing at Becky. "Go on, tell us."

Burpy mumbles something, but I can't understand what he is saying.

"Did you hear that?" Ben asks. "Because I didn't. Can you say it a bit louder, Burpy?"

Burpy goes bright red and shouts at Ben: "He's in prison."

I can't believe what I'm hearing. After everything horrible Burpy has been saying to me, all the time he's forced me to stay away from school, all the upset he's caused Jody, his own Dad is in prison as well.

"What's he in for?" I ask.

"Someone tried to steal his car and he caught them and hit them, it wasn't his fault and the whole thing is really unfair," Burpy says. "But please don't tell anyone."

"I'll tell who I like," I say. Suddenly I feel like I'm floating a mile high, flying. I run off, up the alley and back towards the main road, leaving the twins and Burpy Brad calling after me.

"Where you going?" Ben shouts. "What do you think of Burpy's Dad being in prison?"

"I'm going to school," I shout back, as I disappear round the corner into the main road. Burpy's true story has made me feel so much better, but as I turn back into the main road, I get another shock.

There's Toady. She's the only teacher who has managed to catch up with us.

"What do you think you are doing running away from school like that?" she asks me, turning red with anger.

"Burpy was going to beat me up and no one in school would help," I tell her. I then explain the whole story, from the time Dad was arrested, right up to today.

"It's not your fault your Dad is in prison," Toady says. "It's easy for other people to judge, but I bet if we knew about some of their parents, they wouldn't be great people." Just as she is making me feel better, we reach the school gates and she is called away. A few children in the playground begin their stupid comments about Dad being in prison, but I'm not going to run away this time.

"It's not my fault my Dad is in prison and, anyway, he can be whoever I want him to be," I shout. "You say what you like, I don't care, and I bet your parents aren't as wonderful as you think." I laugh and they are really shocked I seem to be so happy. Without Burpy to get them going, they soon go quiet as I walk to my classroom.

After that, no one says anything nasty about Dad being in prison, but as the days go past, Jody and I can't help wondering how we are going to tell Mum the truth about where Dad is. How can I tell her in a way that will stop her getting upset and annoyed with me? Then, after more than a week, Mum turns up at school to collect Jody and me as usual, except something really strange happens.

"I've got a bit of a surprise," Mum says. "Shall we go for an ice cream?"

"Yes," Jody and I scream.

"Alright, alright, calm down," Mum says. She takes us to the cafe up the road from the school and we are allowed three scoops each – chocolate, strawberry and vanilla. Her surprise must be really important.

"I have to tell you something," she says.

"What?" we ask, nervous she is going to try and get us to do extra homework or something.

"Dad's not in space, or at sea or on a spying mission in Brazil," Mum says. "He's ...," Mum stops and stares at us with a really worried look in her face. Her eyes are all watery and she looks as if she is doing everything she can to stop herself crying.

"He's what?" I ask.

"He's … he's in prison."

"Oh that," I say, as Mum begins to cry.

"We thought you didn't know," Jody says.

"We've known for ages and we were wondering how to tell you," I say. "Don't worry Mum, we're all okay." It feels really good that no-one is pretending anymore, but there's another question that begins to upset me now. "Why did you lie to us?" I ask.

"I'm sorry. I thought it was best," Mum says. "I was only trying to do the right thing. I didn't want you to be disappointed with your Dad and I didn't want to upset you. You know how horrible people can be about this sort of thing."

"Tell me about it," I say, sarcastically. "I certainly found out just how stupid people can be." Jody and I tell her all about the horrible things that have happened at school, and then Mum asks, "How long have you known?"

"Weeks," I say.

"We knew all those silly things you told us about Dad weren't true," Jody says. Then, through her tears and her crumpled-up miserable face, Mum begins to smile and she actually laughs.

"Would you like to go to see him?" Mum asks.

Jody and I both go quiet. Everything has been so weird we can't believe that, in the end, Mum has told us the truth so easily. It was a simple as that, no fireworks. Just a few words and the truth is out there, there are no more lies.

"You must want to see him, don't you?"

"Yes," we both roar.

"Good," Mum says, now smiling and wiping away her tears.

I can't sleep all night and the next morning we set off really early for the drive to the prison. It takes two hours and seems even longer.

"There it is," Mum says, pointing to a huge building like a castle behind lots of fences, wires and walls. The prison officers search Mum and Jody and me as we go in and then we go to this really big room with lots of people sitting round tables, talking and sometimes crying. Mum holds our hands really tight. It hurts. Then, at the other end of the room, we see Dad. He would usually run over as soon as he saw us, but Mum tells us the prison people say he has to stay sitting at the table.

"Hello mate, hello gorgeous,"

Dad says to me and Jody when we get over to him. He gives us all a big cuddle and is smiling in a really strange way. It doesn't look real, and it isn't. He goes quiet and, gradually, as the smile disappears, tears start to flood down his face. Jody and I can't help staring. I've never seen my Dad cry before and I am shocked.

Mum also begins to sob. "We haven't come all this way to blubber," she jokes, as she and Dad start to smile again and laugh just a little bit.

"What have you been doing?" Dad asks Jody and me.

"We've all been telling each other stories," Jody says.

"Stories, what stories?" Dad asks.

Jody tells him all about Mum pretending that he was an astronaut, a sailor and even a spy! The more Dad hears, the more upset he seems, but this time he doesn't cry. He and Mum just look at each other with really sad eyes. I want to speak, but I can't. I can't think of anything to say.

Mum is about to say something, when Jody says, "And the weird thing is that we ended up lying to Mum because we thought she was confused and didn't know you were in prison."

Then, all of a sudden, Dad laughs and after a few seconds we are all giggling. "Well, Mum only pretended because she loves you and didn't want you to get upset," he says, getting a bit serious again. "Now everyone knows the truth and that's good. And it's a good thing you lot managed to get here when you did," he whispers, leaning towards us and smiling. "I've been doing the usual work to find out who the people are here, but I'm

130

131

going to have to stay for a while longer to finish my secret investigations. What do you think, fellow explorers?"

"Well, it all looks pretty weird," I say. "There must be something very valuable in this place for them to build all these fences round it."

Jody and Mum look a bit confused, and then they catch on.

"We've been doing our own research from the base station and we've found powerful radio signals coming from this building," Mum says. "We'll have to study them some more, won't we Captain Jody?"

"Yes, but we'll need to come back here soon as well," Jody says.

Our old Mum and Dad are back. Everything seems better, almost as though it will get back to normal again. Then a bell rings and we have to leave. We all have a big hug together and the prison officer looks a bit annoyed. I don't know when I'll see Dad again or when he'll be coming home, but Mum says she'll take us to see him again soon.

It's just getting dark when we get home. Mum goes upstairs and calls us to come up and get ready for bed. Then, before we can move, she calls us again. This time she sounds excited. "Jimmy, Jody, come here quickly," she shouts from my bedroom. "Look!" she says, as she points out of the window at the birds' nest. All the chicks are flying in and out of the holly bush. It's amazing to see and it would be even better with Dad. I close my eyes and think of him standing beside me. I can't wait to see him, but, until I do, I know exactly where I can find Dad.

THE END

About the Publisher

Action for Prisoners' Families

Action for Prisoners' Families is the national charity supporting the development of services for prisoners' families. It provides information on support services and produces a range of publications and resource material for families and professionals.

Email: info@actionpf.org.uk Website: www.prisonersfamilies.org.uk

Other titles in this series

Danny's Mum

The story of Danny, whose mother is sent to prison. It explores his feelings of loss and confusion. Through friends at school and others, Danny begins to talk about his mum and to look forward to her return.
For children aged 3-6 years.
Illustrated by Lesley Saddington

Tommy's Dad

The story of a young boy and his sister whose father is sent to prison. It explores their feelings of loss, anger and frustration at not being told what's going on, until their mother finally decides to take them to see their dad.
For children aged 4-7 years.
Written by Emma Randle-Caprez and illustrated by Nick Sharratt.

Need help?

The Prisoners' Families Helpline

The Prisoners' Families Helpline is the national helpline supporting the friends and families of prisoners. They can give practical information about visiting and keeping in touch, how the prison system works and many more issues. They can also talk through how imprisonment can affect children and how to support children who have a parent in prison.

www.prisonersfamilieshelpline.org.uk